Little Mouse's
Book of Colors

Written and illustrated
by Julie Durrell

MERRIGOLD PRESS® • NEW YORK
Golden Books Publishing Company, Inc., New York, New York 10106

Library of Congress Catalog Card Number: 90-84470
ISBN: 0-307-59754-7

The sky is gray and it is pouring.
Sitting here is very boring.
I'd like to play outside today.
I think I'll go out anyway.

T. C. MOUSE

Where is my **green** umbrella? I wonder.
I'm not afraid of the rain and thunder.

I'll put on my **purple** socks.
I keep them in this old shoe box.

My big **brown** sweater may be old,
But it will keep away the cold.

I'd like to wear my bright **red** vest.
I found it in this big **red** chest.

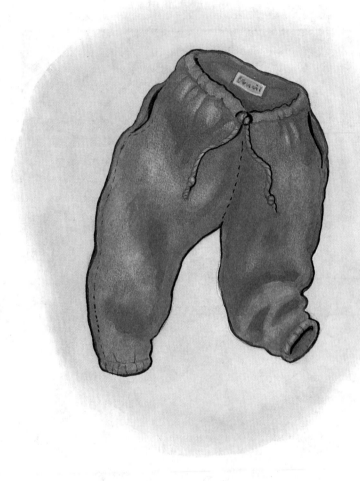

My new sweat pants are **royal blue**.
All my mouse friends want them, too.

My **pink** raincoat I can't forget.
Without it I'd be soaking wet!

In **yellow** boots my feet will stay
Dry and cozy while I play.

This **orange** hat will keep me warm.
And now I'm ready for the storm.

I step outside and close the door,
But it's not raining anymore!

I jump for joy—do you know why?
A great big rainbow fills the sky!

Can you name the colors of the rainbow?